Clifford THE BIG RED DOG®

TUMMY TROUBLE

Adapted by Josephine Page

Illustrated by Ken Edwards

**Based on the Scholastic book series
"Clifford The Big Red Dog"
by Norman Bridwell**

From the television script
"Tummy Trouble" by Lois Becker and Mark Stratton

SCHOLASTIC INC.

New York   Toronto   London   Auckland   Sydney   Mexico City
New Delhi   Hong Kong

No part of this publication may be reproduced, or stored in a retrieval system, or transmitted in any form or by any means, electronic, mechanical, photocopying, recording, or otherwise, without written permission of the publisher. For information regarding permission, write to Scholastic Inc., Attention: Permissions Department, 555 Broadway, New York, NY 10012.

ISBN 0-439-21358-4

Copyright © 2000 Scholastic Entertainment Inc. All rights reserved. Based on the CLIFFORD THE BIG RED DOG book series published by Scholastic Inc. TM & © Norman Bridwell.
SCHOLASTIC, CARTWHEEL BOOKS and associated logos are trademarks and/or registered trademarks of Scholastic Inc. CLIFFORD, CLIFFORD THE BIG RED DOG and associated logos are trademarks and/or registered trademarks of Norman Bridwell.

Library of Congress Cataloging-in-Publication Data available

10 9 8 7 6 5 4 3 2   00 01 02 03 04 05

Printed in the U.S.A.   24
First printing, December 2000

"Today you will do a trick for your treat," Emily Elizabeth said to Clifford.

She held up a treat

for Clifford to sniff.

"Down, Clifford," she said.

Clifford lay down.

Then he sat up,

opened his mouth,

and waited for his treat.

Emily Elizabeth tossed the treat

into Clifford's mouth.

"Good boy," she said.

"Roll over."

Clifford rolled over.

He rolled and rolled.

Then he sat up,

opened his mouth,

and waited for his treat.

Cleo and T-Bone walked by.

"Why are you sitting like that?"

Cleo asked.

"I am waiting for Emily Elizabeth

to give me a treat," Clifford said.

"I did a trick for her."

"I saw Emily Elizabeth

in her mother's car,"

said T-Bone.

"They drove away."

"I will give you a treat,"

said Cleo.

Cleo gave Clifford a treat.

She gave T-Bone a treat.

And she gave herself a treat.

"You have to do a trick

for your treat," Clifford said.

T-Bone stood

on his hind legs.

"That was very special,"

Cleo said.

She tossed a second treat
to T-Bone.

"That was a good toss,"
T-Bone said.

Cleo gave herself a treat

for her good toss.

"You will get sick

if you eat too many treats,"

Clifford said.

"Thank you for worrying

about me," said Cleo.

"That was very special.

You should get another treat."

T-Bone chased his tail.
Cleo tossed him a treat
and gave herself a treat
for her good toss.

Clifford walked

on his front paws.

Everyone got a treat

for that.

Clifford and T-Bone

did many more tricks.

Cleo tossed more treats.

The whole box of treats

was empty!

"Don't worry," said Cleo.
"We still have two boxes
full of treats."

"My tummy hurts,"

said T-Bone.

"Mine hurts, too,"

said Clifford.

"You are probably hungry,"
said Cleo. "Have some
more treats."

Soon two boxes of treats

were empty.

Then three boxes of treats

were empty.

T-Bone lay on his back.

"I'm full," said Cleo,

who had a very big tummy.

"Me, too," said T-Bone,

who had an even bigger tummy.

"Me, three," said Clifford.
He had the biggest tummy
of all.

Emily Elizabeth came back
with treats for Clifford
and his friends.
She saw the three
empty boxes.

She saw the three

sick dogs.

"Poor doggies," she said.

"You shouldn't have

eaten all those treats.

But everybody makes
mistakes sometimes—
even the biggest, reddest,
best dog in the world.
I love you, Clifford."

Do You Remember?

Circle the right answer.

1. One of the animals walked on his or her front paws. It was…
   a. Cleo.
   b. T-Bone.
   c. Clifford.

2. Clifford felt sick because…
   a. he had a cold.
   b. he ate too much.
   c. he ate a bad apple.

Which happened first?
Which happened next?
Which happened last?
Write a 1, 2, or 3 in the space
after each sentence.

Cleo gave Clifford a treat. _____

Emily Elizabeth drove away
with her mom. _____

Emily Elizabeth saw the
three empty boxes. _____

Answers:

Emily Elizabeth saw the three empty boxes. (3)
Emily Elizabeth drove away with her mom. (1)
Cleo gave Clifford a treat. (2)
1-c; 2-b.